7-10

WOODS BRANCH

OUR GALAXY AND BEYOND

NEPTUNE

By Darlene R. Stille

Published in the United States of America by The Child's World®
P.O. Box 326, Chanhassen, MN 55317-0326
800-599-READ
www.childsworld.com

*Content Adviser:
Michelle Nichols,
Lead Educator for
Informal Programs,
Adler Planetarium
& Astronomy
Museum, Chicago,
Illinois*

Photo Credits: Cover: NASA/JPL/Caltech; AFP/Corbis: 13, 16; Corbis: 6 (Christie's Images), 7 (Stocktrek), 11, 17 (Charles E. Rotkin), 18 (Roger Ressmeyer), 19 (Pablo Corral V), 23, 24, 25, 26 (Reuters NewMedia Inc.); Getty Images/Photodisc: 4; Hulton-Deutsch Collection/Corbis: 5; NASA/JPL/Caltech: 8, 10, 14, 15, 21 (USGS), 27, 31.

The Child's World®: Mary Berendes, Publishing Director
Editorial Directions, Inc.: E. Russell Primm, Editorial Director; Dana Rau, Line Editor; Elizabeth K. Martin, Assistant Editor; Olivia Nellums, Editorial Assistant; Susan Hindman, Copy Editor; Susan Ashley, Proofreader; Kevin Cunningham, Peter Garnham, Chris Simms, Fact Checkers; Tim Griffin/IndexServ, Indexer; Cian Loughlin O'Day, Photo Researcher; Linda S. Koutris, Photo Selector

Library of Congress Cataloging-in-Publication Data
Stille, Darlene R.
   Neptune / by Darlene Stille.
      p. cm. — (Our galaxy and beyond)
Summary: Introduces the planet Neptune, exploring its atmosphere, composition, and other characteristics and looking particularly at how humans learned about the gas giant that is four times the size of Earth.
Includes bibliographical references and index.
   ISBN 1-59296-052-9 (lib. bdg. : alk. paper)
   1. Neptune (Planet)—Juvenile literature. [1. Neptune (Planet)] I. Title. II. Series.
QB691.S744 2004
   523.48'1—dc21   2003006335

TABLE OF CONTENTS

CHAPTER ONE

DISCOVERING NEPTUNE

How do you find something that you can't see? If that something is out in space, you can use math. This is what two young **astronomers** in England and France did in the 1840s. At that time, Uranus was the farthest known planet from the Sun. But there was something weird about Uranus. Uranus was not always where it should be. It wobbled as it orbited, or went around, the Sun. What could be causing this odd behavior?

In 1845, English astronomer John Couch Adams thought he had an answer. He thought there might be another planet even farther away than Uranus. The

Uranus was thought to be the planet farthest from the Sun until scientists discovered the smaller Neptune hiding behind it.

At the same time but in different countries, John Couch Adams (above) and Urbain J. J. LeVerrier suspected that another planet might be the cause of Uranus's strange behavior.

unknown planet's gravity could be tugging on Uranus. Gravity is the

force that attracts a smaller object to a bigger one. The Sun's gravity

holds planets in orbit around the Sun. Earth's gravity holds you down

on the ground.

In France, a young astronomer named Urbain J. J. Le Verrier

worked on the same problem at the same time. Both astronomers

Most images of Neptune, the Roman god of the sea, show him holding a three-pronged spear called a trident.

used math to figure out the point where the unknown planet should

be. In September 1846, German astronomer Johann Gottfried Galle

aimed a powerful **telescope** at that point in the sky. Sure

enough, there was a bluish-colored planet that no one had seen

before. Le Verrier named the planet Neptune after the ancient

Roman god of the sea.

GRAVITY

Our solar system is made up of the Sun and the planets, moons, comets, and asteroids that orbit the Sun. But what keeps these many pieces orbiting the Sun? The answer is gravity. There wouldn't be a solar system without gravity. Gravity helped planets form and grow bigger at the beginning of the solar system. Now, it holds those planets in orbit around the Sun. It keeps moons orbiting around their planets, too. Gravity not only works in our solar system. It also holds billions of stars and solar systems together in a group called a galaxy.

You cannot see Neptune without a telescope. It was hard to find because it is so far away. It is an average of 2.8 billion miles (4.5 billion kilometers) from the Sun. The path Neptune takes to orbit the Sun is shaped like an oval, not a circle. So sometimes it is closer to the Sun, and sometimes it is farther away. Neptune is usually the eighth planet

In this multiple image of Neptune's surface, scientists learned that the lightest areas indicate Neptune's higher elevations.

from the Sun. Pluto is usually the ninth planet. But sometimes Pluto comes closer to the Sun than Neptune.

Neptune is big. It is more than four times larger than Earth. Neptune has a diameter of 30,775 miles (49,528 km). Earth's diameter is only 7,926 miles (12,756 km). A planet's diameter is the length of a straight line going through the center of it, from one side to the other.

Neptune is one of four huge, outer planets called gas giants. The other three are Jupiter, Saturn, and Uranus. Neptune is the gas giant farthest from the Sun.

Only one spacecraft, *Voyager 2,* has visited Neptune. *Voyager 2* did not carry astronauts. It flew past Neptune in August 1989. It took pictures and made measurements of the planet. Almost everything we know about Neptune comes from this single visit. As *Voyager 2* came close to Neptune, its cameras saw a beautiful blue ball in space.

A SPACECRAFT NAMED *VOYAGER 2*

The ground around Cape Canaveral, Florida, began to shake. The air filled with a low rumble. Then smoke and fire poured out of a huge rocket on a launch pad. Slowly, the rocket lifted off the ground. Faster and faster it rose into the sky. The big rocket carried a small spacecraft named *Voyager 2.*

In 1977, the United States launched two spacecraft named *Voyager 1* and *Voyager 2.* They were robot space probes. They went to explore the gas giant planets. Both *Voyagers* flew by Jupiter and Saturn. *Voyager 1* did not explore any other planets, but *Voyager 2* went on to study Uranus and Neptune. In 1989, *Voyager 2* reached Neptune. It took many pictures and measurements. After visiting Neptune, *Voyager 2* headed out of our solar system toward other stars. It is still gathering information to send back to Earth.

CHAPTER TWO

NEPTUNE'S ATMOSPHERE

The layer of gases around a planet is called its atmosphere. Neptune's atmosphere is made up mostly of the gases hydrogen and helium. Methane gas high in the atmosphere helps give Neptune's clouds their blue color.

Pictures from the *Voyager 2* space-craft in 1989 showed clouds that looked like blue stripes around the planet. *Voyager 2* also saw three other shapes in the clouds. Scientists named the shapes the Great Dark Spot, the small

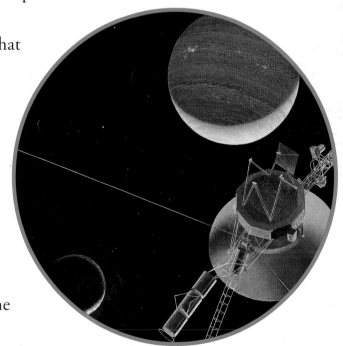

An artist's concept of Voyager 2 *investigating Neptune and one of its moons*

dark spot, and the scooter. The scooter was a small, white cloud that went around Neptune very fast.

The planet Jupiter also has a spot, called the Great Red Spot. Could the Great Dark Spot on Neptune be like the Great Red Spot? Jupiter's Great Red Spot is a storm with swirling winds like a hurricane. Astronomers have known about it for about 300 years, and it could even be older than that!

Neptune's Great Dark Spot is more mysterious. The Hubble Space Telescope, a telescope in orbit above Earth, took pictures of Neptune in 1994. The Great Dark Spot was gone. The small dark spot had also disappeared. But a new Great Dark Spot had popped up in another place on the planet. Scientists do not know what the spots are. They may be holes in the methane clouds above Neptune.

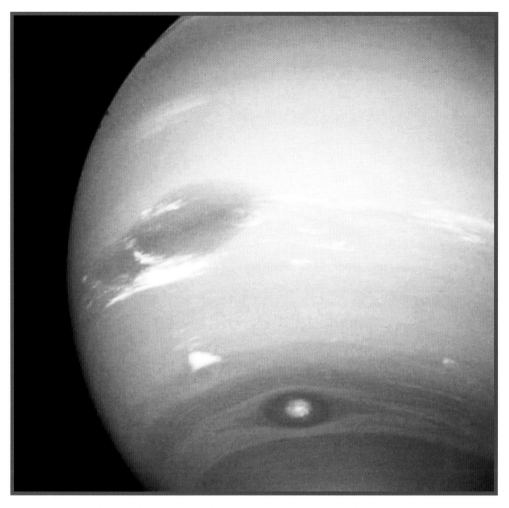

Scientists think this Great Dark Spot on Neptune may be a storm system.
They have not been able to explain why such spots disappear and then
are seen again later on other parts of the planet.

The *Voyager 2* and Hubble pictures showed that the clouds in
Neptune's atmosphere are always changing. Strong winds blow clouds
and storms around. Neptune's atmosphere has the strongest winds of
any planet. They can blow as hard as 1,200 miles (2,000 km) per hour.

CHAPTER THREE

What Neptune Is Made Of

Scientists cannot see through the clouds around Neptune.

They must guess what the planet is like below its atmosphere.

They do know that it is not like Earth. It does not have solid ground

you could walk on. It does not have a surface of rocks and soil.

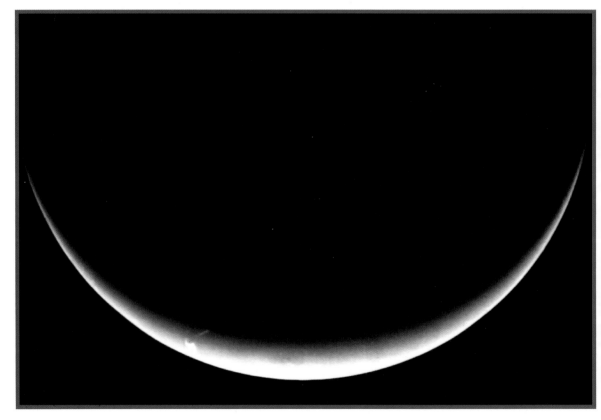

As this image of its south pole shows, Neptune appears firm and solid. But it is really a thick ball of gases that would be impossible to walk on.

Instead, scientists think that Neptune is made of layers. The top layer is Neptune's atmosphere and is made of gases. The gases blend into a liquid layer below called the mantle. The mantle is made of water, methane, and

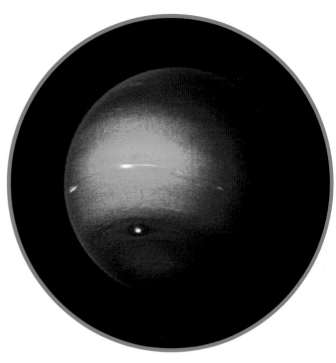

The intense red seen around Neptune's edge in this Voyager 2 *photo is caused by sunlight that hits the planet's methane haze and is reflected back into space. The darker areas indicate regions that absorb more sunlight into the methane.*

ammonia. The liquid mantle is above a solid core at the center of Neptune. The core is made of ice and rock.

Something is heating the inside of Neptune. Even though Neptune is a very cold planet, it gives off about twice as much heat as it gets from the Sun. Scientists would like to find out what is making the heat. This is one of the mysteries of Neptune.

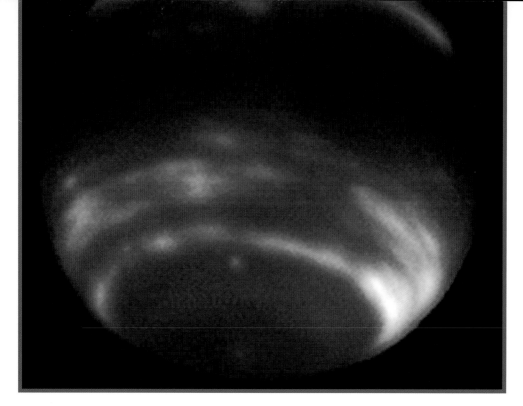

Using the powerful Keck II telescope, the Lawrence Livermore National Laboratory was able to capture images of a major storm (lower right) on Neptune in 1999.

The heat inside Neptune may be warming its mantle. The heat may cause the liquid layer of Neptune to move up, down, and around inside the planet. Heated liquid deep inside the planet might move up to the surface of the mantle. It could warm the bottom layer of the clouds. This would make the top of the clouds cold and the bottom of the clouds warmer. The temperature difference might cause Neptune's strong winds.

CHAPTER FOUR

NEPTUNE THE MAGNET

Neptune acts like a big magnet in space. Earth is also like a

magnet. Earth's core is made of iron. Many magnets are made of

iron. The outer part of Earth's core is probably melted iron.

Scientists think that motions inside the liquid iron make Earth a

The hot liquid iron being poured at this steel mill gives us an idea of what Earth's core probably looks like. This might be what Neptune's core looks like, too.

magnet. But Neptune's core isn't made of iron. It is made of ice

and rock. We do not think of ice and rock as being magnets.

Scientists think that the motions in Neptune's liquid layers make

Neptune a magnet.

*Renowned astronomer Dr. Carl Sagan joined other scientists to study
the information brought back from Neptune by* Voyager 2.

Magnets stick easily to a metal refrigerator because of their magnetic field.

All magnets have an area around them called a magnetic field.

This area is where the magnet's "pull" works. Hold a magnet close to

a refrigerator door. Let go, and the magnet seems to jump to the door.

This is because the door was inside the magnetic field. Hold the mag-

net farther away, and the magnet drops to the floor when you let go

of it. The door was outside the magnetic field. Neptune's magnetic

field is much larger than Earth's magnetic field.

CHAPTER FIVE

THE RINGS AND
MOONS OF NEPTUNE

Scientists know of four rings around Neptune. They are not

as big and bright as the famous rings of Saturn. Neptune's rings

look very dark. At first, scientists thought that they did not go

around Neptune completely. But *Voyager 2* took pictures proving

that they were rings. Scientists think the rings are made of dust

and small rocks.

Astronomers have discovered 11 moons orbiting Neptune.

Neptune's biggest moon is called Triton. It was discovered in 1846,

the same year Neptune was discovered. The second largest moon is

called Nereid. It was discovered in 1949. A moon called Larissa

was first spotted in 1981. Five smaller moons were discovered by

Voyager 2 when it flew by Neptune in 1989. In 2003, astronomers reported finding three more moons around Neptune. They used powerful telescopes and computers to find these three faraway moons.

Triton is the only moon that we know much about. It has a diameter of about 1,680 miles (2,700 km). It orbits about 220,500 miles (354,800 km) above Neptune. *Voyager 2* discovered that Triton has a thin atmosphere. The atmosphere is made of nitrogen and methane.

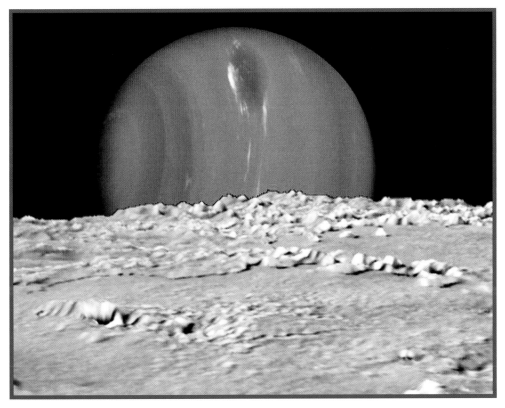

From the rough surface of its moon Triton, Neptune looks like a huge blue bead.

Triton's surface has the coldest known temperature in the solar system. It can drop to –390º Fahrenheit (–235º Celsius). The surface is made mostly of ice. Triton may have some rock in its core. Some parts of Triton's surface are smooth, while other parts are covered with grooves. Many moons have deep holes, called craters, but *Voyager 2's* cameras did not see many craters on Triton.

Scientists think that there may be **volcanoes** or **geysers** on Triton. They are not like those on Earth. Volcanoes on Earth shoot out hot rock. Earth's geysers shoot out hot mud or water. However, Triton's volcanoes and geysers shoot out slushy ice or clouds of icy nitrogen.

Triton orbits Neptune backwards. It goes in the opposite direction of Neptune's orbit around the Sun. This is slowing Triton down. Someday, Triton may break up into smaller pieces or crash into the surface of Neptune.

WHERE DID NEPTUNE'S MOONS COME FROM?

At least some of Neptune's 11 moons may be pieces left over from a gigantic crash in space. A comet or asteroid may have whizzed in from the edge of the solar system. It may have slammed into a big moon orbiting Neptune. The crash may have broken off pieces of the moon. The small moons of Neptune could be these broken pieces.

Triton may have been formed in the big crash, or it may have formed somewhere far from Neptune. Maybe it came close to Neptune and was captured by the planet's gravity. The force of Neptune capturing Triton could have melted ice under Triton's surface. It could have caused Triton to orbit Neptune backwards.

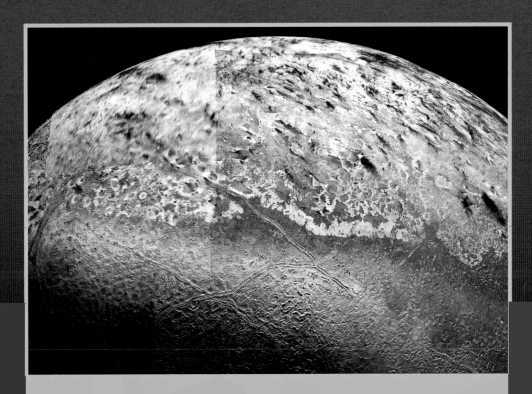

CHAPTER SIX

HOW NEPTUNE
MAY HAVE FORMED

Astronomers have some ideas about how Neptune may have formed. They think that our solar system began as a hot, swirling cloud of gas and dust. The dust was made of tiny pieces of metal and rock. The Sun formed in the center of the cloud. Then the cloud flattened. Astronomers call the flattened cloud a disk.

Pieces of metal and rock came together in the disk near the Sun. The rocky planets—Mercury, Venus,

The planets probably formed in a swirling cloud of dust and gas that may have looked something like this huge mass out in space.

Earth, and Mars—formed in this area. They have surfaces made of

rocks and soil.

In parts of the disk farther

from the Sun, it was colder.

Larger rock and metal cores

formed because they combined

with ice. The gas giant planets—

Jupiter, Saturn, Uranus, and

Neptune—formed in this area.

The large cores combined and

grew larger. Then their gravity

started attracting gas in the outer

In 1994, pieces of a comet struck Jupiter, one of the gas giants. This dramatic happening was captured by the Hubble Space Telescope and was the first time humans had ever seen such a strike.

solar system. As Saturn and Jupiter captured more and more gases,

they grew even bigger.

The solar wind is always coming off of the Sun. The Sun is a hot, glowing ball of gas. The solar wind is made of tiny particles of gas. The gas particles "blow" off the outer layer of the Sun. This outer layer is called the corona.

The solar wind moves at up to 625 miles (1,000 km) per second. In the early solar system, it easily pushed gases away toward the planets. The light gases helium and hydrogen were first blown toward the rocky planets closest to the Sun. These gases were in the atmospheres of the rocky plan-

were small, the force of their gravity could not hold the light gases. Have you ever watched a balloon filled with helium float away? You can imagine how easily the light gases floated away from Earth! The solar wind also pushed the light gases toward the gas giants. However, the force of gravity was strong on the gas giant planets. They were able to capture the hydrogen and helium. Neptune is the farthest gas giant from the Sun. The least amount of gases reached Neptune. That is why Neptune is the smallest of

The planets forming at the very outer parts of the solar system grew at a much slower pace. By the time Neptune had gotten large enough to attract gas, there was not as much gas left to catch. The Sun's energy had pushed most of

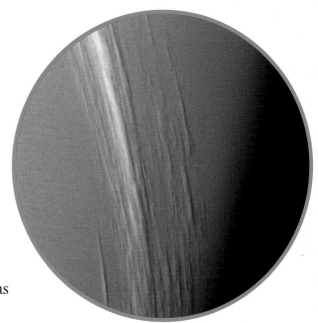

Even though it is the smallest gas giant, Neptune has no shortage of poisonous gases. Some of those gases form the high clouds that look like ridged streaks here.

the extra gas and dust out of the solar system. So Neptune is much smaller than the biggest of the gas giants, Jupiter. Gas giants are made mostly of gas and ice, but they may still have solid cores.

Astronomers have found what they think are disks of gas and dust around other stars like our Sun. They are studying these faraway disks today. They hope to get some clues about how Neptune and the other planets formed in our solar system 4.6 billion years ago.

Glossary

asteroids (ASS-tuh-royds) Asteroids are rocky objects that orbit the Sun.

astronomers (uh-STRAW-nuh-merz) Astronomers are scientists who study space and the stars and planets.

comets (KOM-its) Comets are bright objects, followed by a tail of dust and ice, that orbit the Sun in a long, oval-shaped path.

geysers (GYE-zurs) Geysers are holes in the surface of Earth that hot water and steam shoot out of.

telescope (TEL-uh-skope) A telescope is an instrument used to study things that are far away, such as stars and planets, by making them seem larger and closer.

volcanoes (vol-KAY-nose) Volcanoes are mountains that contain an opening in the surface of a planet. When a volcano erupts, melted rock from pools of magma below the surface spews from the top.

Did You Know?

▸ Triton, Neptune's largest moon, goes around Neptune every six days. Its orbit is shaped like a circle.

▸ Triton is the only major moon in our solar system that orbits in an opposite direction to its planet's orbit around the Sun.

▸ Earth goes around the Sun every 365 days. So an Earth-year is 365 days long. It takes Neptune 165 Earth-years to make one orbit around the Sun!

▸ There are two planets in our solar system you cannot see without a telescope. Pluto is one, and Neptune is the other.

▸ Once every 228 years, Pluto is closer to the Sun than Neptune. Then, Pluto stays closer to the Sun for 20 years. The last 20-year period was from January 1979 to February 1999. Now Pluto will be the farthest planet from the Sun until the 2200s.

Fast Facts

Diameter: 30,775 miles (49,528 km)

Atmosphere: hydrogen, helium, methane

Time to orbit the Sun (one Neptune-year): 164 Earth-years

Time to turn on axis (one Neptune-day): 16.1 Earth-hours

Shortest distance from the Sun: 2.8 billion miles (4.5 billion km)

Greatest distance from the Sun: 2.8 billion miles (4.5 billion km)

Shortest distance from Earth: 2.7 billion miles (4.3 billion km)

Greatest distance from Earth: 2.9 billion miles (4.7 billion km)

Average surface temperature: –353º F (–214º C)

Surface gravity: 1.14 that of Earth. A person weighing 80 pounds (36 kg) on Earth would weigh 91 pounds (41 kg) on Neptune.

Number of known rings: 4

Number of known moons: 11

How to Learn More about Neptune

At the Library

Asimov, Isaac, and Richard Hantula. *Neptune.* Milwaukee: Gareth Stevens, 2002.

Brimner, Larry Dane. *Neptune.* Danbury, Conn.: Children's Press, 1999.

Goss, Tim. *Uranus, Neptune, and Pluto.* Chicago: Heinemann Library, 2003.

Nardo, Don. *Neptune.* San Diego: Kidhaven Press, 2002.

Tabak, John. *A Look at Neptune.* Danbury, Conn.: Franklin Watts, 2003.

On the Web

Visit our home page for lots of links about Neptune:
http://www.childsworld.com/links.html
Note to Parents, Teachers, and Librarians: We routinely verify our Web links to make sure they're safe, active sites—so encourage your readers to check them out!

Through the Mail or by Phone

ADLER PLANETARIUM AND ASTRONOMY MUSEUM
1300 South Lake Shore Drive
Chicago, IL 60605-2403
312/922-STAR

NATIONAL AIR AND SPACE MUSEUM
7th and Independence Avenue, S.W.
Washington, DC 20560
202/357-2700

ROSE CENTER FOR EARTH AND SPACE
AMERICAN MUSEUM OF NATURAL HISTORY
Central Park West at 79th Street
New York, NY 10024-5192
212/769-5100

The Sun
Mercury
Venus
Earth
Mars
Jupiter
Saturn
Uranus
Neptune
Pluto

The solar system

Index

About the Author

Darlene R. Stille is a science writer. She has lived in Chicago, Illinois, all her life. When she was in high school, she fell in love with science. While attending the University of Illinois she discovered that she also loved writing. She was fortunate to find a career that allowed her to combine both her interests. Darlene Stille has written about 60 books for young people.